SCARY FACTS
TO
BLOW YOUR
MIND

Illustrated by Skip Morrow

Written by Judith Freeman Clark & Stephen Long

A New England Publishing Associates Book

PRICE STERN SLOAN
Los Angeles

A New England Publishing Associates Book
Copyright © 1993 Price Stern Sloan, Inc.
Illustrations copyright © 1993 Skip Morrow
Text copyright © 1993 Judith Freeman Clark, Stephen Long,
and New England Publishing Associates, Inc.

Cover Design: Don Brunelle and Skip Morrow

Published by Price Stern Sloan, Inc.,
A member of The Putnam & Grosset Group, New York, New York.

3 5 7 9 11 10 8 6 4 2

ISBN: 0-8431-3580-8

Library of Congress Catalog Number: 93-12249

Library of Congress Cataloging-in-Publication Data

Clark, Judith Freeman.
    Scary Facts to blow your mind by Judith Freeman Clark;
illustrated by Skip Morrow.
        p. cm. — (Facts to blow your mind)
    Summary: Facts, both informative and bizarre, are humorously illustrated.
    Example: a cow can produce sixty-five pounds of manure a day.
    ISBN 0-8431-3580-8
    1. Curiosities and wonders — Juvenile literature. (1. Curiosities
and wonders.) I. Morrow, Skip, Ill. II. Title. III. Series:
Clark, Judith Freemen, Facts to blow your mind.
AG243.C5638   1993
031.02 — dc20   93-12249
                                                         CIP
                                                          AC

Table of Contents

NATURE'S NIGHTMARES

Hold Your Breath!

Did you ever wonder why a beekeeper wears a hat with a veil completely and tightly covering his face and neck? One reason, of course, is to avoid being stung. But it is also because bees are attracted by our breath. So much so, if they could detect the beekeeper's breath, they might swarm right down that person's throat and choke him or her to death!

What A Stinker!

Horror movies often show giant animals or plants that terrorize and kill humans. The idea of being attacked by a monster tomato or eaten by a huge spider is scary, but it's also pretty far-fetched. At least so it seemed until people on the island of Java vowed that they'd actually sighted giant skunks bigger than German Shepherd dogs! They didn't say if they'd been sprayed by the skunks—but someone probably would have noticed if they had!

Killer Catfish

The movie *Jaws* made people wary of shark attacks when swimming in the ocean, but when taking a dip in the rivers of Eastern Europe it's the catfish you have to worry about. This giant catfish known as Siluris glanis, which weighs about 400 pounds, routinely swims to the surface and swallows a duck or a goose. There has been at least one confirmed report of this monster catfish eating a small child in a single gulp!

They're Gaining On You

An average human can run at about 28 miles per hour over a short distance—slightly faster than the speed of a charging elephant. While you might outrun an angry elephant, don't count on getting away from a grizzly bear. These huge animals can run 30 miles per hour and pounce on a person quite easily. The same is true for cheetahs, lions and tigers, all predators that live on fresh meat and can run at least 70 miles per hour. That's faster than the speed limit on U.S. interstate highways!

Surf's Up!

If you go to the beach, better be careful of the surf. And plan to warn your grandchildren, too. Scientists report there's been an increase in the size of waves crashing onto North Atlantic shores. Thirty years ago the waves averaged about 7 feet high. Today most waves are nearly 10 feet high! At this rate of growth, in 200 hundred years "normal" waves may be as high as a two-story house!

Heads Up!

In 1908 an enormous asteroid crashed into the Siberian forests in Russia, plunging to the ground with the force of a 12-megaton atomic bomb and destroying hundreds of square miles of trees. Right now, about 1,000 asteroids—some even bigger than the one that hit Siberia—are spinning out of control in space. One could smash into Earth at any time.

Guess I'll Dig Sand Castles...

Most kids love to go swimming. Even if you can't do a lot of fancy strokes, you probably like to splash in the water. But watch out if you are ever invited to swim in some rivers of South America. There, a bloodthirsty fish known as the piranha is ready to sink its double row of teeth into unsuspecting swimmers. These teeth are as sharp as razors and are used by local natives as arrowheads. Piranhas are among the world's most ferocious fish. They constantly seek the smell of blood underwater. When they find it, piranhas attack their victims without mercy. They're so thorough that they can slice the flesh off a pig in minutes! Better stay on the beach when these fish are at work.

Let's Hot-Foot It Outta Here!

One day in 1943, a farmer in the Mexican village of Paricutin was working in his field. A loud rumbling startled him, and he noticed that thick black smoke was pouring from the ground. In the morning, the farmer's field had disappeared and in its place was a huge cone of ash. Within a few days, his crops had been wiped out by a volcano 450 feet high and over a mile wide. During nearly 10 years of nonstop eruptions, the volcano destroyed the entire village.

Keep The Lid Down

It can be pretty startling when you see a big black rat running along the sidewalk. You may feel safe from rats inside your house, but you'd better watch where you sit. Scientists have proved that rats flushed down a toilet can re-enter your house by climbing back up the sewer pipe!

My Feet Are Getting Wet

Much of Earth is covered by water. And lots more is frozen solid around the North and South Poles. If Earth's atmosphere gets too warm, enough ice could melt to raise the level of the oceans. This increase could be as much as 200 feet if the whole Antarctic ice cap melted. One quarter of existing

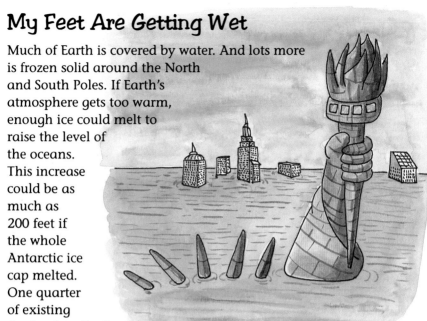

dry land on Earth would be flooded, and cities like London, New York, Tokyo and San Francisco would completely disappear.

I'm Going To The Laundromat

If you want to keep bees be sure your washing machine is working properly. Bee stings leave a smell other bees can detect, and that smell can cling to your clothes unless they are washed thoroughly. The smell sends an alarm to other bees to sting you again and again until you remove the "stinger" smell by washing your clothes!

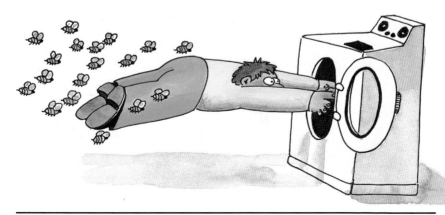

Doctor, Do You Make House Calls?

Maybe you think you can't catch any diseases in a hospital because everything there is kept so clean. Unfortunately, bacteria do manage to slip their way into hospitals. Bacteriologists have found spores of the dread disease tetanus (also known as lockjaw) floating through the air of operating rooms.

Wash After Handling

A certain frog native to Indonesia has highly toxic skin. This poisonous substance is used by local hunters to make very effective darts. The problem is that if a hunter lets the poison get on his own skin it can make him violently ill for days.

You'd Better Pick Up Your Room

The pile of clothes in the corner of your room is a perfect hiding place for brown recluse spiders, whose venom is one of the most potent. Their bite, rarely fatal, can open a wound right down to the bone.

The brown recluse, which is native to the Southwestern United States, may be found in any spot in the home that has been undisturbed for a while—behind furniture, under clothes or in any clutter.

Sleeping Under The Stars

The vampire bat sinks its teeth into a victim to drink blood—and the unwitting prey usually doesn't even know what bit him! This crafty bat waits until its victim (often a cow or other livestock) is asleep, then swoops down quietly from the dark night sky, biting with razor-sharp teeth. Bat spit contains a special chemical that prevents blood from clotting, so the tiny vampire can slurp all he wants, then fly away—leaving the unsuspecting animal a few quarts low.

I'll Get Out Of Your Way

You probably wouldn't have wanted to be around when the Seismosaurus walked by. This dinosaur had four huge legs and a tail that was 75 feet long. Scientists estimate that Seismosaurus was about 150 feet long—one-half the length of a football field!

Hand Me My Shades

The sun is the primary reason there is life on Earth. Without the energy of this life-giving star, nothing could grow. Our world would be barren and cold. Sunlight is so strong that we cannot even look at it directly. If you stare at the sun for more than a few seconds without squinting, the powerful rays will burn holes in the retinas of your eyes!

Not A Friendly Dragon

When a plane crashed on the island of Komodo in 1912, natives told the shaken pilot about a 30-foot dragon in the area that had attacked and killed people. Investigators later found several monster lizards prowling the island.

They were covered with rough, scaly skin, had powerful, chomping jaws, and were seen devouring pigs, deer and dogs!

From Now On, I'm Staying On Shore

A Danish sailing ship of the 1700s once reported a blood-curdling run-in with a giant squid. While cleaning barnacles off the side, three sailors were attacked by a huge creature with arms about 40 feet long. These tentacles wrapped tightly around the men. Two of them were dragged into the water, and the third was freed by his shipmates, who cut off the monster's snake-like arm. When the sailor was pulled to safety, the tentacle was still wrapped tightly around him and had to be sliced off. The other two men were never seen again.

FUN & GAMES

Stay Tuned For The Post-Game Show!

Today, after important basketball games the coaches and star players from both teams shake hands and give boring TV interviews. Several hundred years ago, when the Indians in Central and South America finished playing a game similar to basketball, the postgame show was a little more exciting. In their version of basketball, where a solid ball of rubber was tossed through a hoop, the winners got to keep all the clothes of the people watching the game—and the losing team was executed!

Imagine The Agony Of Defeat!

Looking for a real thrill, sports fans? Probably one of the most hair-raising pastimes in the world, guaranteed to be thrilling to those who participate and those who watch, originated in the Pacific Island nation of Vanuatu. In a ritual activity known as "Gol," men dive headfirst from 100-foot-high towers with their ankles tied to long vines. These prevent the divers from crashing headlong into the ground—most of the time. The tough but stretchy jungle vines, called lianas, are cut to the exact length needed by the diver. The lianas are like elastic bands, so they stretch when the diver jumps. If the lianas stretch too much or if they snap instead, the diver is smashed on impact!

Shake A Leg And Grab A Snake

Dancing played a very important part in the religious ceremonies of the Hopi Indians of America's Southwest. If you were a Hopi Snake Dancer, your dancing was designed to help bring rain, which was essential for growing corn. In the Snake Dance, you wrapped snakes around your arms and neck and even stuffed them into your mouth! If you survived the Snake Dance, you ended it by tossing the serpents to the ground along with some corn meal.

Take Me Out To The Ball Game

When you go to a baseball or football game, you like to cheer for your team and boo the opposition. So did the people of ancient Rome 2,000 years ago. Gladiators performed in armed combat for the pleasure of crowds gathered in huge stadiums who cheered and jeered just as we do today. But the "games" were a little different then. These staged battles pitted teams of gladiators—often slaves with no choice in the matter—against each other or against wild beasts! In some of the grimmest combats, 50,000 people sat and watched as hungry tigers and bears or furious bulls attacked and mauled the gladiators. Many times the gladiators fought without weapons, something the crowds especially enjoyed! Only a few men ever survived these ordeals. But if a gladiator could kill all of his animal or human opponents, he was presented with a wooden sword and granted his freedom.

Airbags Save Lives!

People will try anything—once. As if parachuting isn't scary enough, some people are so crazy they'll jump off a building without a parachute! In August 1984 a movie stunt man named Dan Koko, who leaped from the top of a building in Las Vegas, Nevada, landed on an airbag on the ground 326 feet below him! According to calculations the man was going 88 miles per hour by the time he hit the airbag! There's no news about whether he ever tried the same stunt again!

Sticks And Stones May Break My Bones

For hundreds of years the Surma people of Ethiopia have enjoyed a sport-like custom called "donga." The men gather in groups divided according to village, carrying 6-foot-long hardwood sticks. The best fighters attack each other, trying to knock down their opponents with the sticks. Injuries are common because the fighters don't wear armor—only cotton wrappings around their heads, necks, and arms. Many fighters are scarred badly from past dongas, but killing an opponent is against the rules. If one fighter does kill another, he and his family are banished from the village and they lose all their property. The donga's purpose is to settle disagreements and bring honor to the village. Not only does killing an opponent shame the neighborhood, it guarantees the next stick-fighting session will be bloodier than usual.

Sure, I'll Wear A Batting Helmet

Nolan Ryan, Roger Clemens and a number of other major league pitchers can throw a baseball at a speed of over 100 miles per hour. Imagine standing up to the plate and trying to get a hit off them—or trying not to get hit by one of their pitches while you stand 12 inches or so away from their target of home plate. A baseball thrown at 100 miles per hour can break bones. If it hits you, at the very least you will end up with an incredible bruise in which you can see the imprint of the seams that hold the baseball together.

Watching On TV Is Safer

In Europe, sports fans get so excited about football, the sport that Americans call soccer, that there have been riots over soccer games. The worst soccer-related disaster happened in 1989, when 95 people were crushed to death trying to enter a stadium in Sheffield, England for a game. A crowd of about 4,000 fans rushed the stadium, squeezing the people ahead of them against metal fences that would not budge from the weight. Another 200 people were injured.

I Feel High!

A lot of kids know how exciting it is to jump off a diving board, even one that is only a few feet from the water's surface. Diving headfirst takes a little more skill and courage. If you want to see the world's most courageous divers, head for Acapulco, Mexico. At a special place on the coast called "La Quebrada," these men regularly dive headfirst from a rocky cliff almost 88 feet up—about as high as a nine-story office building. They risk crashing into the stony cliff wall as they go down and face even more danger entering the water, which is only 12 feet deep!

When The Going Gets Tough, The Tough Get Going

All athletes have to train hard, but some football coaches make practice seem like prison camp. Coach Paul "Bear" Bryant took 100 or so members of the Texas A&M team to Junction, Texas, for football camp one summer. All but 29 left by the end of the 10-day camp because they got injured or they couldn't put up with the brutal workouts in 100-degree temperatures. Many players became dehydrated, sweating off 20 pounds in a single day and then spent their "free" time barfing and feeling terrible. Coach Bryant must have felt badly about treating his players so harshly. Before he died he set up a $100,000 scholarship fund for the children of players who survived that horrible football camp— even though the team won only a single game that season.

Don't Let Your Babies Grow Up To Be Cowboys

Modern-day cowboys compete in rodeos where they show off riding and roping skills. It's all dangerous, but the most treacherous rodeo event is bull riding. The cowboy holds a rope tied around the animal's neck, hoping to stay on its back while the bull thrashes around and tries to throw him off. One of the meanest bulls of all time was Red Rock, a one-ton beast that had bucked and knocked 308 would-be riders off his back before champion rider Lane Frost stayed on for the required eight seconds. Even though he was the best rider in the world, Frost was gored later by another bull which turned on him and stuck a horn right through the cowboy's heart!

Take A Deep Breath

Scuba diving can be fun, but William Lamm found it can also turn into a nightmare. In June 1989, Lamm was diving near Florida's St. Lucie Nuclear Power Plant when he was suddenly sucked into an underwater tunnel that feeds water into the cooling system of the nuclear reactor. Dragged through the darkness at 50 miles per hour, Lamm's wet suit was ripped to pieces and he could barely use his scuba tank. Battered against the side of the concrete tunnel as he hurtled along, Lamm thought he was a goner. But, as suddenly as his unplanned quarter-mile journey began, he was tossed up, safe and reasonably sound, into a deserted overflow pond near the power plant.

Take A Walk On The High Side

The twin towers of New York City's World Trade Center stand 110 stories high and 130 feet apart. The year after the building opened, a French performance artist strung a cable between the two towers and—as thousands of people gaped up from the street below—walked across with only a 1-inch cable between him and the pavement 1,368 feet below!

I Dare You

What if your father dared you to sail around the world all by yourself? Tania Aebi was 18 years old when she sailed out of New York Harbor all alone, even though she had never sailed anywhere solo. Her 27,000-mile trip took 2 1/2 years. She survived seasickness, hurricanes and a collision with a tanker. She was the youngest person to ever sail around the world alone—and all because her father dared her to do it!

Now That's Persistence

Climbing high mountains is one of the most difficult and dangerous sports. You scale cliffs of ice, sleep in a thin tent pitched on steep slopes or narrow ledges, and sometimes crawl on hands and knees through fog or blinding snowstorms. In 1980, a German climber named Reinhold Messner crashed through a thin snow bridge on Mount Everest, the world's highest mountain, and fell into a crevasse. He spent hours carving steps in the icy walls so he could escape a frozen coffin. His solo journey through waist-high snow up the 29,000-foot peak was a real endurance test. He carried all supplies on his back, used no oxygen tanks, and he traveled without radio, climbing ladder or rope! Reaching the summit, he vowed to continue his mountain conquests. By 1986 he'd scaled all 14 peaks on Earth that are higher than 26,000 feet!

Between A Rock And A Hard Place

If you're claustrophobic, don't take up spelunking, or cave exploring, as a hobby. Spelunkers often have to squeeze through passages as small as 12 inches wide. The floors of many caves are inches deep in water, and tunnels sometimes have only small ledges for walking on. One woman spelunker told how one of her caving mates' helmet batteries lost power—which meant the rest of her underground journey would be a lot more dangerous. Later, on the way out, the spelunkers balanced on a 6-inch-wide shelf, leaping across a huge chasm so they could reach the last part of the ledge leading up, and out into the sunshine.

Oh, Let's Do It Just One More Time

One young man talked his skiing buddy into going up the chair lift for one last run before the ski area closed up for the night. Unfortunately, the ski lift attendant didn't see them hop on and turned off the lift for the day, stranding the two boys in midair half-way up the mountain. The temperatures quickly dropped well below freezing, but the young skiers were too high up to jump to the ground and ski down. They were found half-frozen on the lift at four o'clock the following morning and had to be rushed to the hospital to be treated for frostbite.

YOU WON'T FEEL A THING

I'll Just Take An Aspirin For My Headache

Most of us will never need to have brain surgery, but if we did, we'd want it done by a team of highly trained doctors in a high-tech medical center. That's not the way it's always been done. The practice of brain surgery dates back thousands of years when the medical techniques and instruments weren't highly developed. Stone Age doctors used sharpened sticks and pointed drills made of rock to bore into the skulls of companions who suffered head injuries. Of course, there wasn't any anesthesia to put you to sleep during the brain surgery. What's surprising is that many of the Stone Age patients apparently survived the operation just fine!

A Step In The Wrong Direction

One of the world's worst beauty treatments was given to young girls from rich families in ancient China. They endured a painful procedure in the name of beauty: foot binding. Chinese men believed tiny feet were attractive and also thought women should stay close to home. Because of this, the feet of little Chinese girls were wrapped in tight bandages. Since young bones are soft, they can be bent, folded and squeezed together into a small stump. But it did hurt, and it took several years of binding to ensure the desired results. Chinese women who went through foot binding could hardly walk, because their feet were no more than 3 or 4 inches long!

Early Retirement

On the Isle of Java in the 16th century, people too old to work were sold in the marketplace by their children. The buyers then killed the unfortunate old-timers and cooked them for supper.

Doctor Ants

When tending to cuts or wounds, Brazilian natives sometimes use ants to close the opening in the skin! A species, called "doctor ants," have vise-like jaws that are used to fasten the edges of a wound almost the way a staple holds paper together. The ants' bodies are taken off but the heads are left in place to help the cut heal tightly!

Just Pull The Plug

During the 1940s and 1950s, doctors found they could control patients who acted crazy or became violent by cutting away the front part of a person's brain. The result of this irreversible operation, called a frontal lobotomy, is quiet, almost robotlike, behavior. Unfortunately, the patients never regained control of their personalities and could not think well or clearly ever again. Gradually, doctors stopped doing lobotomies, but not until about 50,000 people had been "lobotomized" and doomed to spend the rest of their lives with only part of their brains functioning.

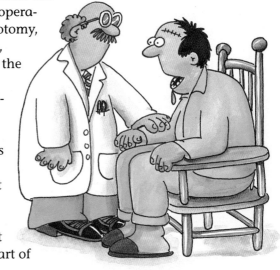

Quick, Call A Witch Doctor

Magic can literally scare a person to death. The victim suffers no physical harm but is simply pointed at by an enemy during a frightening voodoo ceremony! Totally convinced that something horrible is about to happen, the victim often screams and falls to the floor in terror, before finally crawling off to bed and eventually dying from his or her own fears.

It's Called The Graveyard Shift

If you are lucky, you'll never be an emergency room patient. If you do break a bone or get a gash on your head, just hope that it doesn't happen at 4:00 a.m. in July. Researchers say that's the worst time to be treated in a hospital emergency room. The doctor on duty will probably be an intern who has just graduated from medical school a month before and hasn't seen many patients. Besides being inexperienced, the new doctor will be trying to stay alert and awake, because young interns have to work 14 or more hours a day, many of them at night.

Could I Have An Extra Blanket?

In Lithuania 100 years ago some mothers had an unusual way of guaranteeing that newborns would grow up healthy. A Lithuanian mom fearful for the future health of a new baby would wrap it up warmly and put the baby to sleep in a graveyard overnight. Babies surviving this "health insurance" ritual were thought to be easily able to live to adulthood.

MENAGERIE OF MONSTERS

Travelers, Beware!

If you ever get the urge to hike through the Himalayan mountains, watch out for the abominable snowman! This enormous wild man is described as being about 15 feet tall and is possibly a meat-eater! Although nobody has ever photographed one, many natives in the region are convinced that the creature exists. Hundreds of people who live in the Himalayas say they have seen the abominable snowman, sometimes called a yeti, and pictures have been taken of the yeti's footprints.

All Right, I'll Get Dressed

In medieval times, people were afraid of werewolves. One way a werewolf could regain human form was simply to put his clothes back on. But if he didn't want to be human again, he would be forced to drink a potion made of devil's dung while being burned and beaten by young girls with tree branches.

I Could Go For Some O-Negative

Are you sure there's no such thing as a vampire? In the United States the Vampire Research Center keeps records on about 600 people who, it claims, really are vampires. About 80 percent of the folks on the list are women—each with an urge to drink blood during the full moon.

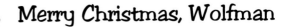

Merry Christmas, Wolfman

Some kids born on Christmas feel frustrated because their birthdays get forgotten in the excitement of the holiday. It was worse in medieval Europe to be born on December 25. It was believed then that these people were actually werewolves. Those suspected of being one of these monsters often were disposed of by being burned at the stake.

Not Just A Tall Tale!

Many people claim to have seen and even photographed the Sasquatch, a 500-pound monster found in Canada and the Pacific Northwest. Hundreds have reported close encounters with this 7-foot, hairy, apelike creature also known as Big Foot. Miners have fought with groups of Sasquatches in Washington, and a California farm wife and her children fled to a nearby forest when the muscled monster crashed into their home, apparently looking for a meal. In the 1920s, a Canadian camper said he was grabbed by Big Foot, carried in his sleeping bag to the animal's lair, and held for a week before being able to escape the Sasquatch's clutches!

BEHAVE, OR ELSE!

Crime Doesn't Pay

When the Egyptian ruler Tutankhamen died in 1323 b.c., his body was buried with hundreds of precious objects and hidden deep inside a many-layered and well-guarded tomb. Not too many years later, robbers thought they could outsmart the guards by digging through the walls without getting caught. The would-be thieves were captured, beaten mercilessly, stuck through the middle with sharp stakes and, finally, sealed up inside the burial chamber and left to die a slow death. Their remains were found there more than 3,000 years later when the tomb was excavated by British archaeologists in 1922.

Guilty, Your Honor

In ancient Tibet the guilt or innocence of accused criminals was determined by the following test. The person had to put his hand in a pot of boiling oil, into which a white stone and a black stone had been tossed. If the person pulled out the white stone and did not burn his arm, he was innocent.

Count Off By Tens

In Roman times, it was customary to punish unruly military troops by "decimating" them. This meant killing every tenth soldier, even if only a few misbehaved.

Reporting For Duty, Sir!

It wasn't easy to get out of military service in ancient Babylon. If someone didn't show up when he was ordered to report for duty, the king would hunt him down and cut his head off. The severed head then would be displayed in public as a warning to other reluctant recruits.

Obey The Law, Or Else

The Code of Hammurabi, the laws of the Babylonians, dates from the year 1750 b.c. The code spelled out the punishments for all sorts of crimes. Anyone taking property during a fire was to be thrown into that fire alive. If a son hit his father, the son's hand was to be cut off. If a slave struck a gentleman, the slave's ear was to be cut off. If a surgeon performed an operation but was unsuccessful in treating his patient, the surgeon's hand was to be cut off.

No Wonder Columbus Left

Around the time Columbus sailed on his voyage of discovery, Spain was in the midst of a brutal investigation of anyone thought to be less than 100% faithful to the Catholic Church. During what was called the Inquisition, you could be thrown in prison without a trial and then tortured until you confessed, even if you had done nothing wrong. After your confession, you might be drawn and quartered, hung or burned at the stake—all in the name of the Church.

FRIGHTENING FOLKS

They Won The Battle And The War

In 1598, the English explorer John Manwaring encountered the Persian ruler Shah Abbas I returning from a raid against an enemy in the northern part of his Central Asian country. Each of the 1,200 horsemen accompanying the Shah carried the head of an enemy stuck on the end of his spear. The warriors also wore the ears of their enemies, cut off and strung on cords around their necks.

I'll Just Get A Job Washing Windows

You probably wouldn't have wanted to work for the Roman Emperor Caligula. He was known for having extremely violent tendencies. Once, the emperor ordered a man who was in charge of the Imperial gladiators to be beaten. After the man had been whipped with chains for several days, Caligula decided to have him killed. The man's head had been badly injured in the beating and Caligula didn't like the resulting smell.

Maybe I Don't Really Love You

In Russia during the 1660s, Stenka Razin—the leader of a tribe of warriors called Cossacks—was famed for his ferocious ways. He kidnapped the beautiful daughter of a Persian ruler and then fell in love with her. Later, when drunk, Razin decided that the Volga River—on which he often traveled through central Russia—was jealous of the princess. The fierce Cossack threw the young woman into the river as a sacrifice. Her clothing was covered with heavy embroidery and jewels, so she immediately drowned.

Do You Mind Sharing My Cup?

People living near southern Russia during ancient times generally avoided their neighbors, the Scythians—and with good reason. These fierce tribesmen delighted in scalping and killing enemy soldiers but saving their skulls. Scythian warriors scooped out the brains of their dead foes and made drinking mugs from the skulls. They hung the mugs on their belts and kept them handy for that special drink of blood and water.

A Captive Audience

Kenneth Neu wanted desperately to be a nightclub singer, but his career as an entertainer was going nowhere. You wouldn't think that murdering a theater owner would improve his chances, but it did give him an opportunity to sing for an audience. He tap-danced along Death Row and serenaded the rest of the convicted murderers. One of his favorite songs was "I'm fit as a fiddle and ready to hang."

Population Planning

While driving though the town of Cuba, New Mexico in 1958, a prospector named Norman Foose decided there were just too many people in the world and it was up to him to do something for the cause of population control. He took out his rifle and shot two people, explaining to police that there's not enough food for everybody and he was just helping to even the balance.

A Real Perfectionist

A career criminal, Carl Panzram had no remorse for any of the 21 murders and thousands of other crimes he committed. When he was standing on the gallows about to be hanged for his life of crime, he was unimpressed by the skills of the hangman. "Hurry it up," he snapped, "I could hang a dozen men while you're fooling around."

Want To Go Shopping?

It wasn't very glamorous to be a woman warrior among the ancient Sarmatians. They fought with spears, wore animal skins and were considered very good at attacking and destroying their enemies. The Greek historian Herodotus wrote that Sarmatian girls were encouraged to be as bloodthirsty as possible. They probably didn't have many boyfriends. Before they were allowed to marry, they had to have killed a man in battle.

Dear Diary

When Graham Young was released from prison for poisoning his father and stepmother, he took a job at a factory. Soon, more than 70 of his coworkers became ill with a mysterious illness. After two died, police began to suspect poison, and they questioned the recent parolee. Young swore he was innocent, even though police found poison in his possession along with a diary naming all his victims. He claimed his diary simply contained notes for a novel he was writing.

OCCUPATIONAL HAZARDS

What Goes Up Must Come Down

Going to the top floor of a skyscraper and looking down at the street makes most of us dizzy just from thinking about falling. Yet, some construction workers called steeplejacks can walk on an 8-inch-wide girder 1,000 feet above the ground, look down and hardly notice the 100-story drop. They avoid looking up though. Seeing moving clouds above them could make them lose their balance!

My Master Is Better Than Your Master

In ancient Asia, slaves would do anything for their masters—even kill themselves. It was customary for a slave to give a long speech praising his master and, when finished, the slave would take a large sharp knife and slash at his throat, cutting his own head completely off.

I Love School

You think going to school every day isn't much fun? Consider this. Back in the 1800s, children as young as 7 or 8 had to work as chimney sweeps instead of attending classes. Only small children could fit inside most chimneys. Many died at a young age from lung diseases due to spending so much time cleaning out the inside of dirty, soot-filled chimneys.

Bring Me Up Nice And Slow

The bends, or nitrogen narcosis, is a painful, paralyzing condition that occurs when the pressure inside a person is higher than the outside air pressure. When a deep-sea diver rises to the surface too rapidly, his or her body can't adjust quickly enough from the higher pressures underwater. This causes tiny nitrogen bubbles to build up in the blood and body tissue. These bubbles clog the veins and arteries so that the heart, brain, and joints cannot get enough blood. If a diver can't be quickly put into a decompression chamber to restore the balance between inside and outside pressure, the diver can die as the nitrogen bubbles expand and cut off the blood supply.

Let's Run Away From The Circus

In circus families, children often join the family act at a young age. In the Wallenda family this meant joining the family's tightrope act. The "Flying Wallendas" performed all over the world, walking across a wire suspended high in the air between two platforms. Their speciality was a formation in which they walked across on each other's shoulders, the smallest child on top. Karl Wallenda introduced his children and grandchildren to the high wire, and the family kept the act going. Five family members died during the act, which was performed without safety nets of any kind.

Asleep At The Wheel

A plane flying across the Pacific Ocean to Seattle, Washington one night a few years ago mysteriously drifted into Canadian air space. Air traffic controllers tried to make radio contact with the crew but got no response. The Canadian Air Force was called in and they flew toward the plane and found out what was wrong. The flight crew was sound asleep! The Air Force shined lights into the cockpit of the wandering plane and woke up the crew, avoiding an almost certain crash landing.

How About A Desk Job?

Scientists usually study "quiet" volcanoes, but sometimes disaster results if eruptions occur without warning.

Six vulcanologists were crushed or burned to death when Mount Galeras, in the Andes of Colombia, exploded with lava, ash and red-hot boulders. The men were standing in the crater when the eruption began. One scientist got out alive, but he had a broken jaw and fractured skull. Both of his legs were broken, too, as he tried to outrun the rain of rocks and debris. The scientists were at Mount Galeras studying ways to lower the death toll resulting from natural disasters.

How Does This Thing Work?

A young woman walking down the street heard a voice coming from the back of a garbage truck. She looked up and saw a man's head squeezed between the jaws of the compactor. He pleaded with her to push the lever on the side of the truck to release him from his tight trap. She found the lever and pushed it. The compactor opened and the garbage truck driver safely climbed out. Only then did she discover that had she pulled instead of pushed the two-way lever, the compactor's jaws would have closed and crushed the man to death.

Cued To Puke

Do you get scared when you have to stand up and give a report in class? That feeling in the pit of your stomach is called stage fright, and even many professional entertainers suffer from it. Some of them are so scared about appearing before the public that they puke just before going onstage. Usually, their fear goes away once they begin to perform.

That Guy Is A Real Live Wire!

Metal ladders may be light and easy to move around, but the old-fashioned wooden ones have at least one big advantage. They don't conduct electricity. Every year construction workers, roofers and house painters get deadly shocks when their metal ladders come in contact with live wires!

LET'S SKIP THIS

Water, Water, Everywhere

Humans cannot safely drink salty ocean water even though they can swim in it, dive under it and sail on it. If you were stranded on a desert island with no fresh water and you became thirsty enough to drink ocean water, you would grow even thirstier. The salt would take away what little moisture you have in your body. You would grow weak, and if you kept on drinking saltwater, you would go insane.

Are You Dead Yet?

Imagine having someone you thought was dead come to life right in front of you. In 1878, this happened when a young girl in New Jersey apparently died of a heart attack. She was put to rest in her coffin and her family paid their last respects, kneeling before her lifeless body. Her father, upset over the loss of his daughter, buried his head in his arms and cried. Imagine his shock when he looked up and saw his daughter moving toward him, reaching her arms around him for a hug! The girl had awakened from a coma. She then shuddered and fell over, dead for the second—and last—time, and was immediately buried.

Curiousity Can Kill People, Too

Some people stop to take a look when they see a road accident. Such rubber-necking can be dangerous because onlookers can hinder the efforts of rescue workers or become victims of an even bigger accident. When a trailer truck overturned in Phang Na province, Thailand, a crowd gathered to take a look. Unfortunately, the trailer's cargo was dynamite. When it exploded it killed 122 people whose curiosity had gotten the better of them.

Can I Have A Glass Of Water?

Death Valley, California is hot and sandy. Pioneers often traveled through it in search of a shortcut to the easy life on California's coast. Much to their terror they learned too late that Death Valley is well-named. Daytime temperatures go above 130 degrees and the waterholes are full of undrinkable, chemically contaminated alkaline water. People who ran into trouble crossing Death Valley's 150-mile stretch went crazy from the heat, digging for water or walking in circles until they dropped from exhaustion and died.

Is There Light At The End?

Underground tunnels can be scary to ride through, especially those that pass under water. Fortunately, most tunnels aren't really that long, so the trip is over fairly quickly. Some train tunnels, however, are so long that you wonder whether you'll ever see the other end. Japanese railway trains stay underground for 33 1/2 miles when passing through the Seikan tunnel, the longest in the world.

Close Encounters

Do you believe Unidentified Flying Objects—UFOs—really exist? A 1978 survey reported that about 20 million Americans claimed to have seen a UFO. Many told of actually meeting alien beings or having been "beamed up" to space ships. In 1961, a man and woman said they were kidnapped by space aliens while driving one night along a New Hampshire country road. Under hypnosis, the couple described their terrifying experience, convincing many who listened that the kidnapping had really happened. Between 1970 and 1979 alone, 160 people reported they had been kidnapped and held on UFOs in the United States alone!

Did You Doublecheck Your Math?

Engineers who design and build long suspension bridges have to use very complex mathematical formulas to ensure the bridges won't fall down. The Tacoma Narrows Bridge in Washington state was brand-new in 1940 when it collapsed after the wind hit the bridge just right (or just wrong). Because of a mathematical miscalculation, the bridge began to shake and vibrate so much that its heavy steel cables swung around like jump ropes. The bridge took a couple of hours to collapse—a good thing for the people driving across! Many cars had to be abandoned, but all the people ran to safety before the bridge sank into the water.

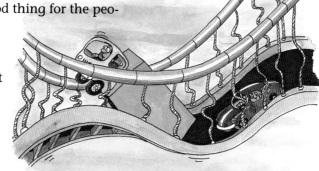

Better Say Your Prayers

Sometimes it's better to say your prayers before going to church. Some churches in the southern United States encourage people to hold rattlesnakes as they worship, and to drink strychnine, a deadly poison! After such practices began in the early 1900s, a number of men and women died after snakes wrapped around their necks and bit them. Others died from gulping poison out of paper cups while singing and praying!

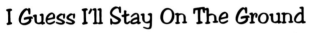

I Guess I'll Stay On The Ground

Visiting the top of the Empire State Building can be fun, but not back on July 28, 1946. An Army bomber got lost in thick fog and smashed into the skyscraper, killing the pilot and 12 other people, many of whom were on the observation deck staring in terror as the aircraft headed straight at them.